LITTLE SIMON

An imprint of Simon & Schuster Children's Publishing Division • 1230 Avenue of the Americas, New York, New York 10020 • First Little Simon paperback edition October 2021 • Copyright © 2021 by Simon & Schuster, Inc. All rights reserved, including the right of reproduction in whole or in part in any form. LITTLE SIMON is a registered trademark of Simon & Schuster, Inc., and associated colophon is a trademark of Simon & Schuster, Inc. For information about special discounts for bulk purchases, please contact Simon & Schuster Special Sales at 1-866-506-1949 or business@simonandschuster.com. The Simon & Schuster Speakers Bureau can bring authors to your live event. For more information or to book an event contact the Simon & Schuster Speakers Bureau at 1-866-248-3049 or visit our website at www.simonspeakers.com.

Series designed by Laura Roode.

Book designed by Chani Yammer. The text of this book was set in Usherwood.

Manufactured in the United States of America 0921 MTN 10 9 8 7 6 5 4 3 2 1

Cataloging-in-Publication Data is available for this title from the Library of Congress.

ISBN 978-1-5344-8715-4 (hc)

ISBN 978-1-5344-8714-7 (pbk)

ISBN 978-1-5344-8716-1 (ebook)

the adventures of

SOPHIE MOUSE

18

The Hidden Cottage

By Poppy Green • Illustrated by Jennifer A. Bell

LITTLE SIMON

New York London Toronto Sydney New Delhi

Contents

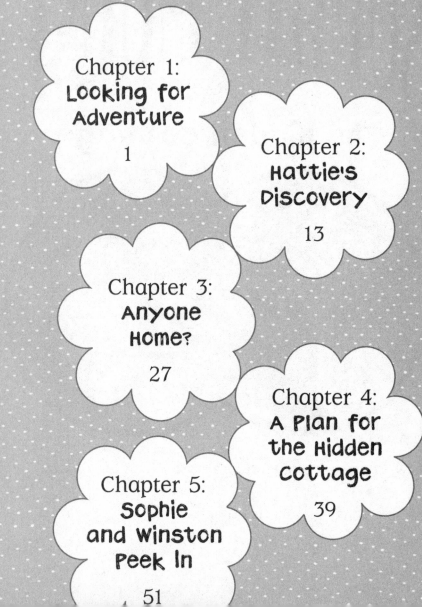

chapter 1

Looking for Adventure

Sophie Mouse's whiskers twitched. The autumn sun was warming a frosty chill on her nose. The morning had been frigid—an early blast of the cold winter that was to come.

But now, at Forget-Me-Not Lake, it was almost warm enough for Sophie to take off her coat.

She and Hattie Frog helped their friend Owen Snake lower his leaf boat into the water.

"Finally!" Owen exclaimed. "I thought I'd never get this thing done."

"You've worked so hard on it,"

Sophie said encouragingly.

"It looks beautiful!" Hattie remarked.

Hattie was right. Owen had used red and orange maple leaves and yellow birch leaves. The boat was so colorful.

"I just hope it's watertight!"
Owen said.

Sophie and Hattie held the boat
steady. Owen slid carefully into it
and sat down.

"Ready?" Sophie asked. "One, two, three!"

She and Hattie pushed the boat out onto the water.

Owen stared at the bottom of the boat, watching for leaks. A smile spread across his face. "It's completely dry!" he called over to his friends.

"Hooray!" Sophie cheered.

Hattie clapped and jumped up and down.

They watched Owen paddle around for a few minutes. Then he stopped. His tail

drooped and his smiled faded.

"What is it, Owen?" Hattie called. "Don't you like your boat?"

Owen sighed. "I do," he replied glumly. "It was pretty exciting not knowing . . . would my boat sink? Would it float? But what now?"

Owen paddled to shore.

"Do you ever wish we could have more . . . *adventure*?" he asked Hattie and Sophie.

Hattie frowned. She didn't look too sure about adventure. She was usually pretty careful to *avoid* adventure, actually.

But Sophie fondly remembered some of their adventurous times.

There was the time they followed a trail of huge paw prints that led to a shy baby bear!

And the time they found the glowing crystal cave!

And the time they went in search of emerald berries in mysterious Weedsnag Way!

Sophie thought for another moment. Come to think of it, they had found their biggest adventures *outside* Pine Needle Grove.

Maybe that was the key to finding their next one.

"I have an idea," Sophie said to her friends. "Let's take a hike!"

chapter 2

Hattie's
Discovery

"Yeah! Let's do it!" cried Owen.

But Hattie was more hesitant. "A hike to where?" she asked.

Sophie shrugged. "We could head out toward Birch Tree Slide," she said. "Maybe we could explore around Butterfly Brook. We could find some spots we've never been."

Hattie crossed her arms. "What if

we get lost?" she asked. "We would
need to take a map. And water."

Sophie nodded. Hattie was always
so cautious. But she was right.

"How about this?"
Sophie began. "I'll go
get supplies at
my house. Owen,
you come with

me. And since we might see some birds on the way, Hattie, you could go get your binoculars."

Hattie's face lit up. She loved bird-watching. "Great idea!" Hattie exclaimed. With that, she ran off to get her binoculars.

"Meet us at my house!" Sophie called after her.

Sophie and Owen headed to the huge oak tree. Nestled in the roots was the Mouse family's house. Sophie's dad, George Mouse, was in the kitchen making lunch.

"Hello, Owen," Mr. Mouse said warmly. "Hi, Sophie. How was the lake today?"

Sophie raved about Owen's leaf boat. Then she explained their plan to go on a hike.

"Sounds like fun," Mr. Mouse said. "Want me to make sandwiches for you to take with you?"

Mr. Mouse pulled out some sandwich fixings: oat nut bread, cashew butter, and raspberry jam.

Meanwhile, Sophie ran upstairs to get her sketchbook. *Maybe I'll even find inspiration for my next painting on this hike,* Sophie thought.

Before long, Hattie arrived. She had a map in one hand. Her binoculars hung on a strap around her neck.

Sophie grabbed her satchel. She put her sketchbook inside. She added a water canteen and the sandwiches.

And then they were off.

They hit the trail and headed
north, away from the village.

The trail twisted and turned. The
animals scampered over pine tree
roots. They continued on through a

grove of birch trees. The sun shone
through the yellow leaves and made
them look as if they were glowing.

"What a perfect day for a hike!"
Sophie exclaimed.

Owen led the way. Sophie followed, carrying the map. Hattie came last. Every twenty paces or so, she stopped to listen for bird songs. She'd peer up into the trees through her binoculars. Then she'd hurry to keep up with Sophie and Owen.

The trail rounded a bend. It ran alongside a shallow stream. Then it turned again and ran under a canopy of yellowing ferns.

They clomped up a small rise and down the other side.

Suddenly Hattie called out. "Wait! Did you hear that?"

Owen and Sophie stopped and turned. "Hear what?" Sophie asked eagerly.

Hattie held her binoculars to her eyes. She was looking up into the branches. "A bird! Like a too-wit, too-wooo!"

Owen shook his head.  "I didn't hear it," he said. "Can you see what kind of bird it is?"

Hattie groaned. "Aw, I just missed it! It flew away." Hattie's shoulders slumped and she began to lower the binoculars.

Then suddenly she perked up.

"Wait!" Hattie said. She was looking through her binoculars again. But they weren't pointing up. They were pointing straight ahead. Then Hattie gasped. "What is *that*?"

chapter 3

Anyone Home?

Sophie and Owen came to stand at Hattie's side. "What do you see?" Sophie asked.

Hattie put the binoculars down. "It looks like . . . a cottage!" she cried.

Hattie handed the binoculars to Owen. He aimed them where Hattie was pointing.

"Yes!" said Owen. "It's a little

house. Wow, how did you spot that, Hattie?"

Owen offered the binoculars to Sophie. She looked through the eyepieces.

At first, Sophie couldn't see anything but leaves. "I don't see . . ."

Sophie scanned a bit to the left. Then a bit to the right.

There!

She saw an arched wooden door. Above it was a circular window. They seemed to be set in a stone wall.

But the rest of the cottage was hidden by tree branches.

"It isn't on the map," Sophie said. She pointed to their location.

"I've definitely never seen it before," Hattie agreed.

"It's so tucked away off the trail," said Owen. "You could pass right by and never know it's there."

Sophie looked back and forth between them.

"I say we take a closer look!" she declared.

Sophie didn't wait for her friends to respond. She headed toward the cottage.

Owen followed.

Hattie hung back. "Wait," she called after them. "That's probably someone's house!"

But Sophie didn't hear her.

Sophie cleared the path. She moved branches aside. Her ears were perked up, listening for any sounds in or around the cottage.

But except for their own footsteps, all was peaceful and still.

They came out on the bank of the stream—the same one the trail had run alongside earlier.

On the other side of the stream was the cottage. Now they could see the whole thing. It was small, with stone walls and a thatched roof. A front garden was fenced in by a row of sticks.

It was cozy and sweet, Sophie thought. It had certainly been some-one's home at one time.

But now? That was hard to tell.

The garden was overgrown. The jasmine and clematis flowers were in bloom. But their vines had grown over other plants. A few fence posts had fallen under their weight.

Sophie could see broken spots in the roof. She wondered if water leaked in when it rained.

A water bucket next to the stream was cracked. The handle was rusty. Was it just worn? Or had it been sitting unused for a long time?

"This stream would be perfect for water sliding!" Owen announced. He dipped his tail in the water.

Sophie took in the pretty scene. It looked as if it was right out of a painting. In fact, it would make a great painting!

Hattie came up next to Sophie. "Sophie," she said, "we don't know if someone's living here or not."

Sophie cupped her paws around her mouth. "Hello?" she called out across the stream. "Is anyone home?"

Sophie, Hattie, and Owen stood still, waiting, listening.

There was no reply.

chapter 4

A Plan for the
Hidden Cottage

Sophie really wanted to go inside the cottage, but she didn't feel totally right about it. So the friends turned and made their way back to the trail.

They decided to loop back a different way. As they walked, Hattie saw two gold finches. They came to a clearing—a perfect spot for lunch! They ate their sandwiches on top

of some sunny, warm rocks. Then they made a big loop around to Silverlake Elementary School. They went through the tunnel of honey-suckle and on toward home.

It wasn't the biggest adventure ever. But it *had* been exciting to find the mysterious cottage.

At dinner, Sophie told her mom, dad, and her little brother, Winston.

"It wasn't on the map," Sophie said. "But it was the cutest little cottage. Right across a stream. The garden was wild but pretty."

Sophie's mom looked at her dad. "Who was the chipmunk who used to live out that way?"

Mr. Mouse tugged his whiskers. "I can't remember her name," he replied.

Mrs. Mouse smiled. "She was so kind."

Mr. Mouse passed around the sweet potatoes. "She moved away, I think. To be closer to her grand-chipmunks."

Sophie scooped sweet potatoes onto her plate.

"So the cottage is . . . empty?" Sophie asked them.

Mrs. Mouse shrugged. "I suppose," she replied.

Sophie frowned. That seemed sad. She imagined it was once neat and tidy and picture-perfect. But it had been left to the woods and the weather. Sophie thought about the broken spots on the roof and the overgrown yard.

It wouldn't take much to make it good as new again.

"Mom? Dad?" Sophie said. "Would it be okay if I tidied up the cottage—with Hattie's and Owen's help?"

Her parents looked at each other. Mr. Mouse nodded.

"I don't see why not," he said. "If it's really been abandoned."

Mrs. Mouse had a twinkle in her eye. "Actually, Sophie, I think you are on to something."

Mrs. Mouse told them about a rabbit family in town. The mother rabbit had come into Mrs. Mouse's bakery the other day and got to talking with Mrs. Mouse. It turned out

that Mrs. Rabbit's home had been
wrecked in the terrible rainstorm the
week before, and she needed to find
a new place to live.

"And she has three baby bunnies,"
Mrs. Mouse said. "She brought them
by for treats too. I just feel terrible
that their home got ruined."

Mrs. Mouse looked at Sophie.

Sophie's eyes lit up. She understood what her mom was getting at.

"If we fix up the cottage, we could offer it to the Rabbit family!" Sophie cried. "Just in time for winter!"

Mrs. Mouse nodded.

Next to Sophie, Winston suddenly piped in. "Can I help?" he asked.

Sophie hesitated to answer. On the one hand, it was fun to have a project with her friends—just her friends.

But on the other hand, Winston was very handy.

"I'll ask Hattie and Owen," Sophie said at last.

Winston crossed his arms in a huff.

"But I think they'll say yes," Sophie added.

Winston beamed. "Hooray!"

chapter 5

Sophie and Winston Peek In

Early the next morning, Sophie felt a *pat-pat-pat* on her mattress. Still half-asleep, she opened one eye.

Winston was standing at the side of her bed.

Sophie shut her eye again. "Winston," she said sleepily, "it's Sunday morning. Why are you up already?"

Pat-pat-pat. Winston tapped on her mattress again.

"The cottage," Winston whispered. "Can I see it? Can we go there? This morning?"

Sophie groaned.

But then she opened her eyes. She propped herself up on her elbows.

"Are you really that interested?" Sophie asked.

Winston nodded excitedly.

Sophie couldn't help smiling. She didn't blame him. And she kind of wanted to get another look herself.

So Sophie agreed and got dressed. She and Winston went downstairs and each had a bowl of cereal.

After breakfast, they left a note saying where they were going. Then Sophie led Winston through the woods to the cottage.

She stopped him on the bank of the stream. As she had the day before, Sophie called across to the house.

"Hello? Anyone home?" Sophie's voice echoed off the cottage's stone walls.

Again there was no answer.

Sophie and Winston looked at each other. "Just wanted to be sure," Sophie said.

Then they hopped across rocks to the other side of the stream. They stepped up to the front door.

Sophie raised her paw to knock.

Knock, kn—

The door opened a crack.
Winston gasped. Sophie
took a step back.

"Um, hello?" Sophie
said bravely.

But there was no one there. Sophie realized it was her knock that had pushed the door open.

"Hello?" Sophie called one more time. She opened the door all the way.

Now they could see the whole interior.

A little wooden bed in one corner was unmade. Two stools next to a table were overturned.

On the wood-burning stove stood a rusty teakettle. Jars of nuts and berries and seeds lined a shelf.

Dirty dishes were piled in the sink.

The floor needed sweeping. And every surface in the cottage was covered with a layer of dust.

"Definitely no one here," Winston said.

Sophie nodded. "Not for a very long time."

She walked over to an easel. On it was an unfinished painting of a waterfront.

Wow! thought Sophie. The scene was incredibly detailed. Benches dotted a boardwalk. Boats were tied up along the docks. A jetty of rocks jutted out into the water. At the end were the beginnings of a lighthouse—but the brushstrokes gave way to blank canvas.

Whoever had lived here was an artist. Just like Sophie!

Sophie looked down at the easel shelf. A paintbrush, still loaded with paint, was stuck to the palette. The paint had dried long ago.

— chapter 6 —

All Paws on Deck

On Monday morning, Sophie and Winston arrived early at Silverlake Elementary.

They were just in time. Hattie and Owen were walking up the steps of the schoolhouse.

"Owen! Hattie!" Sophie called to them.

This was her chance to tell them

about the cottage—before they all went inside. Sophie waved them over to talk.

"Guess what!" Sophie began.

She told Hattie and Owen everything her parents had said. All about the chipmunk who used to live in the cottage. And how she'd moved away.

"So no one is living there?" Hattie asked.

Winston nodded. "We went inside it yesterday!" he blurted out. "It looked like no one had been there forever!"

Owen's eyes went wide. "You went *inside*?" he cried.

"What was it like?" Hattie asked.

Sophie described the dustiness and the mess. "It could use a little help," she said. Then she smiled. "So what do you say?"

Hattie and Owen looked confused. "Wait. What?" asked Hattie.

Sophie told them about the Rabbit
family. Then she explained her mom's
idea to help them. "If we fix the place
up, they can live there," Sophie said.
Hattie and Owen loved that idea.
"When do we start?" Owen asked.

Winston stepped into the middle of the group. "I am free next Saturday," he said.

Sophie giggled. Hattie and Owen laughed too.

"Um, is it okay if Winston helps?" Sophie asked them.

Hattie and Owen nodded. "Of course!" Hattie said.

"It sounds like we have a lot of work to do," Owen said. "We can use all the help we can get!"

All week long, Sophie gathered cleaning supplies: dusters, mops, soap, a bucket. Winston made sure his toolbox was in order. He could handle most fixes with his hammer or screwdriver.

SOAP

On Friday, Lily Mouse was excited when she came home from the bakery. She had seen Mrs. Rabbit. "I mentioned the cottage," Mrs. Mouse said. "She looked so hopeful! I'm sure she'll want to see it. Maybe we can take her there next week."

Uh-oh, thought Sophie. Now they had a little bit of a dead-line for their project. Could they get it done that quickly?

Finally, the weekend arrived.
Sophie and Winston packed up their
supplies. They met Hattie and Owen
at the cottage.

They found it unchanged: dishes
in the sink, bed unmade.

"Let's start with dusting," Sophie
suggested. "Everywhere. Then we
can figure out specific chores."

She ran a dust cloth along the easel shelf.

Sophie paused and stared at the painting. She leaned in to look more closely.

Had that sailboat been there before?

And the lighthouse at the end of the jetty—Sophie could have sworn it wasn't that tall last time.

But how could that be? No. She had to be remembering it wrong.

Sophie laughed at herself and kept on dusting.

~ chapter 7 ~

Getting to Work!

Hattie was the most organized of all of them, so everyone agreed she should assign the tasks.

She put Owen in charge of the sleeping area. He would wash the linens in the stream. Then he could hang them to dry in the sun.

"Maybe when I'm done," Owen said, "we could make three more little beds for Mrs. Rabbit's baby bunnies?"

Sophie gasped. "What a great idea!" she exclaimed.

Hattie asked Winston to look around the cottage for needed repairs.

"You could start with the door latch," Sophie said. She remembered how it had opened when she knocked.

Winston nodded. "I'm on it!" he declared.

Hattie assigned herself to the kitchen. She would wash the dishes, clean out the pantry, and wipe down the shelves.

"After that, I'll wash all the windows," Hattie decided.

Finally, Hattie put Sophie in charge of sweeping the floors and tidying the bookshelves.

OWEN:
SLEEPING AREA

WINSTON:
REPAIRS

HATTIE:
KITCHEN

SOPHIE:
SWEEPING AND
BOOKSHELF

"Oh yes," Sophie replied. The books needed a complete reorganization. Many of the books had their pages facing out. Others were in messy piles on the floor.

The friends worked busily for a while. Sophie's sweeping kicked up a lot of dust indoors. So they propped open the front door and all the windows. A lovely breeze blew through. Just the fresh air and sunshine made the cottage feel cleaner and brighter.

Then they all took a break outside. Owen splashed around in the stream. Winston rolled up his pant legs so he could wade.

Sophie and Hattie sat on a grassy patch under the clothesline. The drying bed linens waved in the breeze.

After their break, they decided to focus on the front garden. Hattie trimmed back the overgrown vines. Winston weeded. Owen added some leaf mulch around the rosebushes.

"My mom says keeping them warm over the winter makes them healthier in spring," Owen said.

Sophie snipped a few flowers from the trimmed-off vines. Then she found a vase in the cottage and filled it with water from the stream. She arranged the flowers in the vase.

"Won't this look nice on the table?" Sophie asked.

She led the way back inside. They all agreed the flowers were a perfect homey touch.

Then Hattie started on window-washing. Owen and Winston drew plans for some bunny-size beds.

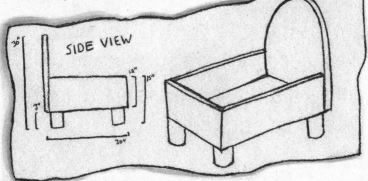

Sophie started sorting the books. Many of them were art books. And what interesting titles.

100 Great Chipmunk Artists

Upcycled Acorn Art

And best of all, *The Color Cookbook*.
Sophie could not resist flipping
through that one. She gasped as she
began to read it. It was an entire
book on how to mix paint colors—
all from things found in nature!

Sophie was completely lost in the pages.

She got so lost, in fact, that she didn't hear the footsteps coming up the pathway. And she didn't hear someone drop a basket in the open doorway.

But she jumped at the sound of a voice.

"What are you doing to my cottage?"

— chapter 8 —

charlotte chipmunk

Sophie hurriedly put back the book she was holding. Hattie gasped. Owen dropped his pencil. Winston rushed to hide behind Sophie. Though he peeked out to get a look at the animal standing in the doorway.

She was an older chipmunk, not much taller than Sophie. She wore a little knit bonnet on her head. Her brown cloak was tied at the neck with a red ribbon. And she held on to a twisted walking stick. A few acorns had spilled out of the basket at her feet.

"Your . . . your cottage?" Sophie asked sheepishly.

"Yes!" said the chipmunk. "My cottage!"

"We . . . we didn't think anyone lived here," Sophie said nervously.

"At least, not anymore. It didn't *look* like anyone lived here. I mean . . ." Sophie was fumbling for her words.

She looked around at her friends. Hattie looked totally embarrassed.

"We're so sorry!" Owen blurted out. He moved toward the door. "We'll leave right away!"

But the chipmunk held up her hand as if to stop him.

She looked around the cottage.

"My kitchen!" she cried. "The dishes are gone. The bed linens are gone."

Sophie tried to explain. "We cleaned—"

"Yes!" the chipmunk interrupted. "You have cleaned. That much is clear. It's never, ever looked so neat in here! I'm amazed."

The chipmunk smiled. Sophie sighed with relief. Maybe they weren't in so much trouble after all.

"Now then," the chipmunk went on, "let's start with names, shall we?"

"I'm Sophie Mouse and this is my brother, Winston," Sophie began.

Owen introduced himself, then Hattie shyly did as well.

The chipmunk nodded. "Well, my name is Charlotte," she said. "And I believe I have met your parents, Sophie and Winston. It was quite a while ago, when I lived here full-time."

Sophie thought for a moment. Did that mean Charlotte still lived here . . . just not all the time?

"We thought you had moved away," Sophie admitted. "We didn't think anyone lived here anymore."

Charlotte nodded. "Well, now *that* makes a bit more sense," she said with a laugh. "But I still don't quite understand. *Why* are you cleaning my cottage?"

"Well, you see, we had an idea," Sophie began.

Then she stopped. She felt a knot tighten her stomach.

The Rabbit family!

Sophie didn't know what to say. They were fixing up the cottage . . . so another family could move in? To Charlotte's home?

Oh dear.

The Rabbit family *couldn't* move in.

How would they explain it? To Charlotte? And to Mrs. Rabbit?

chapter 9

What's the Big Idea?

Charlotte was waiting. Waiting to hear about Sophie's "idea."

"We . . . we . . . ," Sophie stammered. "Well, when my parents said you had moved away, we thought it was sad. Sad that such a lovely place would be abandoned."

Sophie left out the part about the Rabbit family.

Winston stepped out from behind Sophie. "So we thought *we'd* fix it up!" he exclaimed.

Charlotte chuckled. "This place does need a bit of fixing, doesn't it? My grand-chipmunks live all the way over in Rosebush Ravine, so I spend a lot of time over there."

Charlotte looked around the cottage wistfully. "I love this place. I have so many memories here. So I come back every season or so. Whenever I need a little peace and quiet."

She explained that she'd arrived at the cottage the night before.

"I had a lovely quiet evening working on my painting." Charlotte gestured toward the easel.

Aha! thought Sophie. That explained the new details she'd noticed.

"And this morning I've been out gathering acorns," Charlotte said. "I thought I might do a little baking while I'm here."

Sophie thought that might be their cue to go. "We should leave you to your peace and quiet," Sophie said. "We're so sorry. We won't bother you again."

Sophie, Winston, Hattie, and Owen headed for the door.

"Wait!" Charlotte said.

The friends stopped and turned.

Charlotte sat down at her spotless table. She smelled the flowers in the vase. "You really have done a lovely job," she said.

"Thank you," said Hattie. "Actually, we weren't quite done," she admitted.

"Yes," said Sophie. "I was just getting started on the bookshelves."

Charlotte sat silently, deep in thought. She tapped her walking stick on the stone floor.

At last, Charlotte spoke. "I think you've shown me that I need a caretaker," she said. "Someone who can look after the place when I'm not here. Someone who will treat it like their own home."

Charlotte squinted at them.

"Would you four be interested?" she asked.

Sophie looked at her brother and friends. Were they thinking what she was thinking?

A thrill of possibility ran through Sophie. Maybe this could work out for everyone after all: Charlotte, Sophie and her friends, *and* the Rabbit family.

— chapter 10 —

A Picture-Perfect Ending

Sophie's easel was set up next to the coneflowers. She made some purple brushstrokes on the canvas for petals.

"That looks wonderful, Sophie!"

It was Charlotte. She was set up nearby, painting the clematis flowers in her front garden. Charlotte loved to paint as much as Sophie.

Over the last week, the two had become painting buddies. Charlotte lent Sophie her copy of *The Color Cookbook*. They had experimented with new recipes for paint colors.

The two were painting while the Rabbit family explored the cottage. They were going to be live-in

caretakers until their new home was finished! Then, Sophie and her friends would check on the cottage from time to time while no one was living there. Charlotte told the young animals that they could use the cottage whenever they wanted—not just for check-ins!

But before the Rabbits moved in, everyone was helping to really fix up the place.

Winston and Mr. Mouse were patching the broken spots in the thatched roof.

Hattie and Mrs. Mouse were
hanging the café curtains they had
made for the front windows.

Owen had rearranged river stones
to make a little waterslide in the
stream. He was showing Mrs. Rabbit's
bunnies how to slip and slide down
the rocks.

The next day, Charlotte would be heading back to Rosebush Ravine. Before she left, she asked Sophie for a favor. It was a request for just one home improvement.

"I'll come back to visit next season," Charlotte said. "And when I do, I'd love nothing more than to see one of your paintings hanging inside."

Sophie was so flattered. Right away, she knew exactly what she would paint.

The End

the adventures of
SOPHiE MOUSE

For excerpts, activities, and more about
these adorable tales & tails, visit
AdventuresofSophieMouse.com!

If you like Sophie Mouse, you'll love

the adventures of
SOPHIE MOUSE